W9-ALL-603

E SHRAYA
Revenge of the raccoons /
35000097975998

New Haven Free Public Library
133 Elm St.
New Haven, CT 06510

REVENGE OF THE RACCOONS

Written by
VIVEK SHRAYA

Illustrated by
JULIANA NEUFELD

Owlkids Books

We're furry, we scurry, we're wild . . . you worry!

We come for your
doughnuts.

We come for your **cash**.

We come for your **drugstores.**
We come for your **trash.**

We get in your **green bins**.
We poop on your **grass**.

We scratch through your **screen doors.**

We come for your **cats**.

We're **furry**,
we **scurry**,

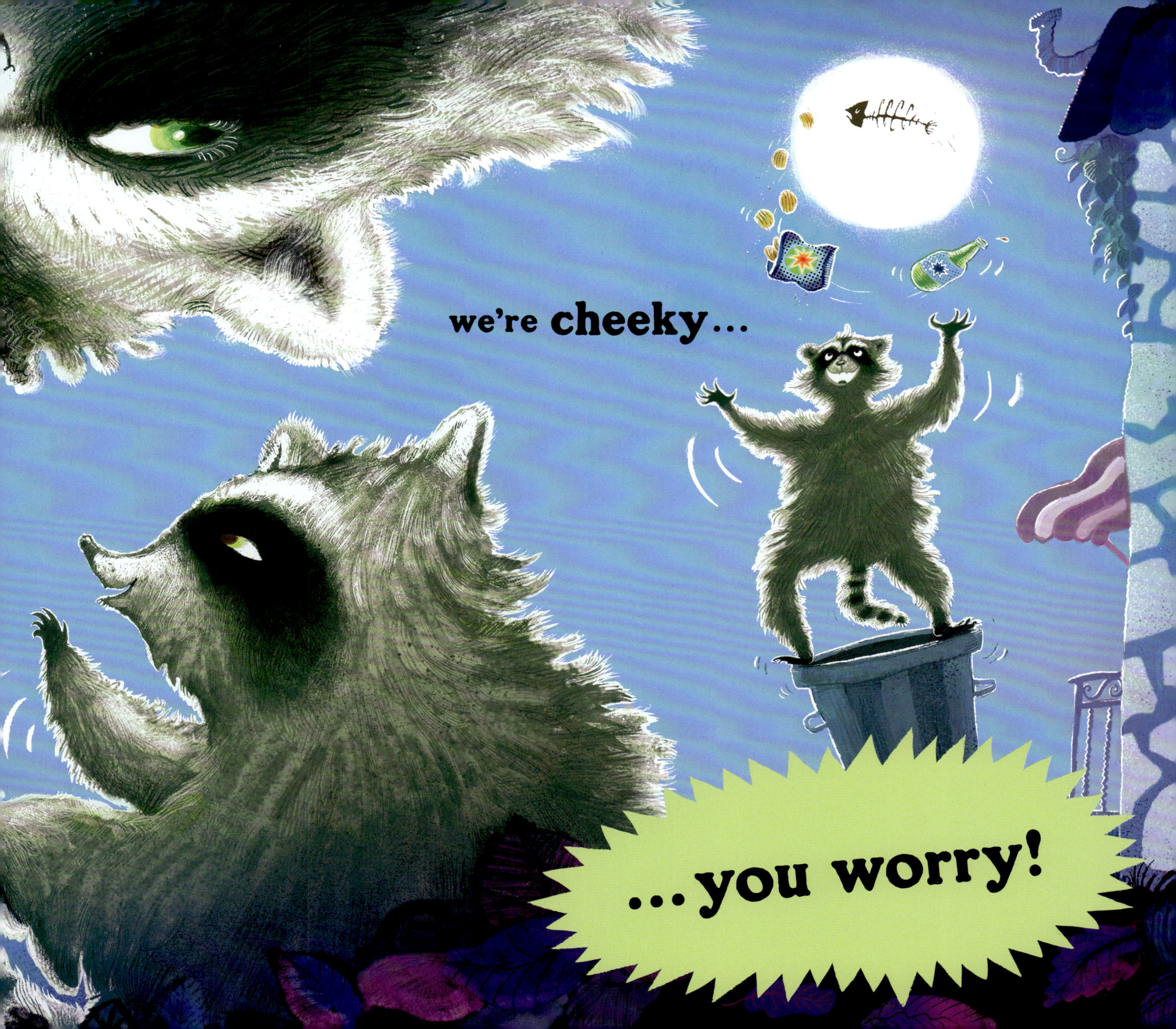
we're cheeky...
...you worry!

We chew on your **fences**.
We crawl up your **trees**.

We climb on your **rooftops** and down your **chimneys**.

We hop on your **subways**.

We swing on your
cranes.

We scale up your
towers

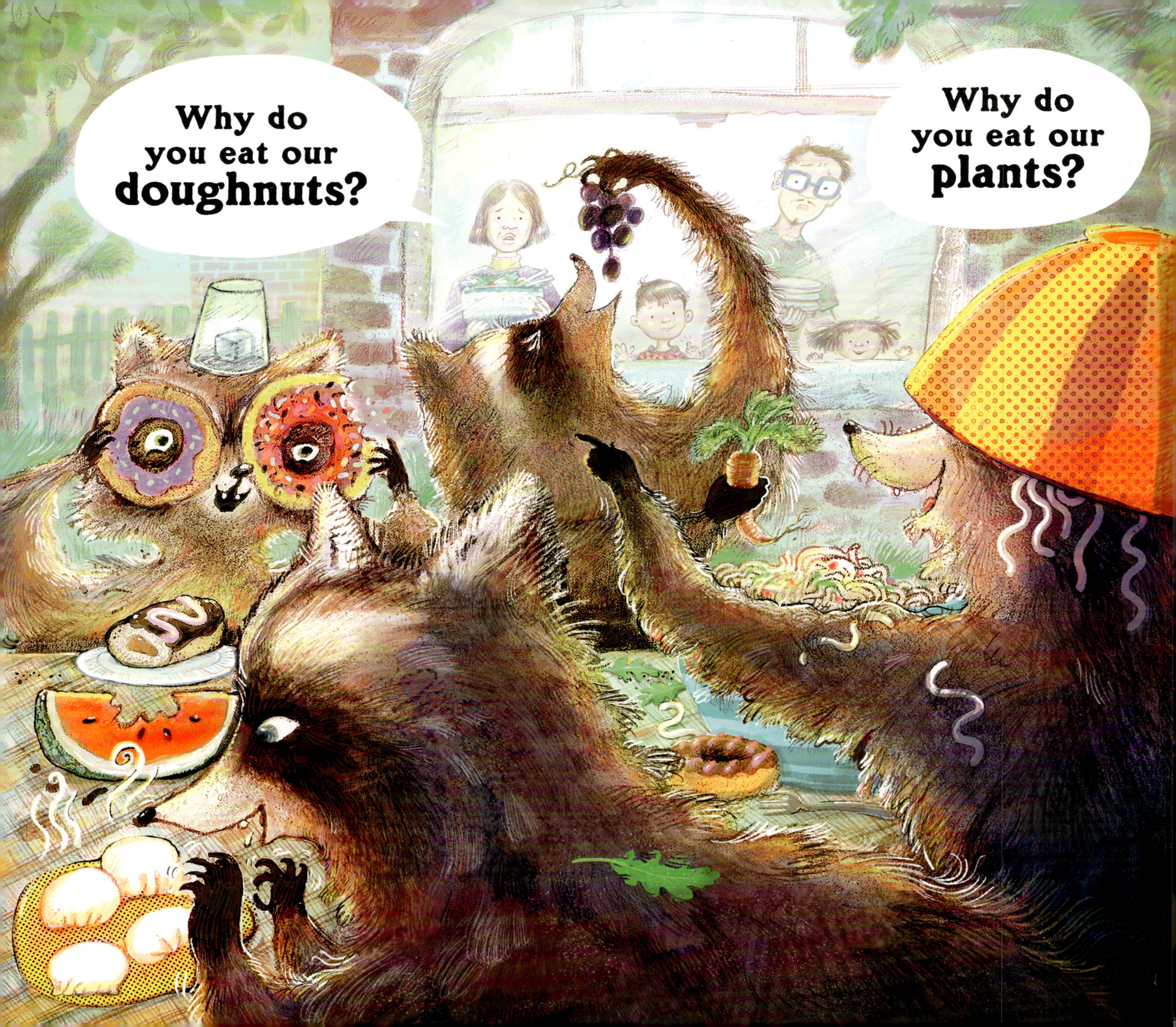
Why do you eat our doughnuts?
Why do you eat our plants?

Do you want to eat **US** next,
then do a **zombie dance?**

Oh, you **silly humans!**
We're glad you asked at last.
You've been careless oh so long!
We've come to right the past...

It was **YOU** who came for **US**,

and built houses everywhere.

But we're not gonna **go away.**

We've come to **make you share!**

We're **furry**, we **scurry**,

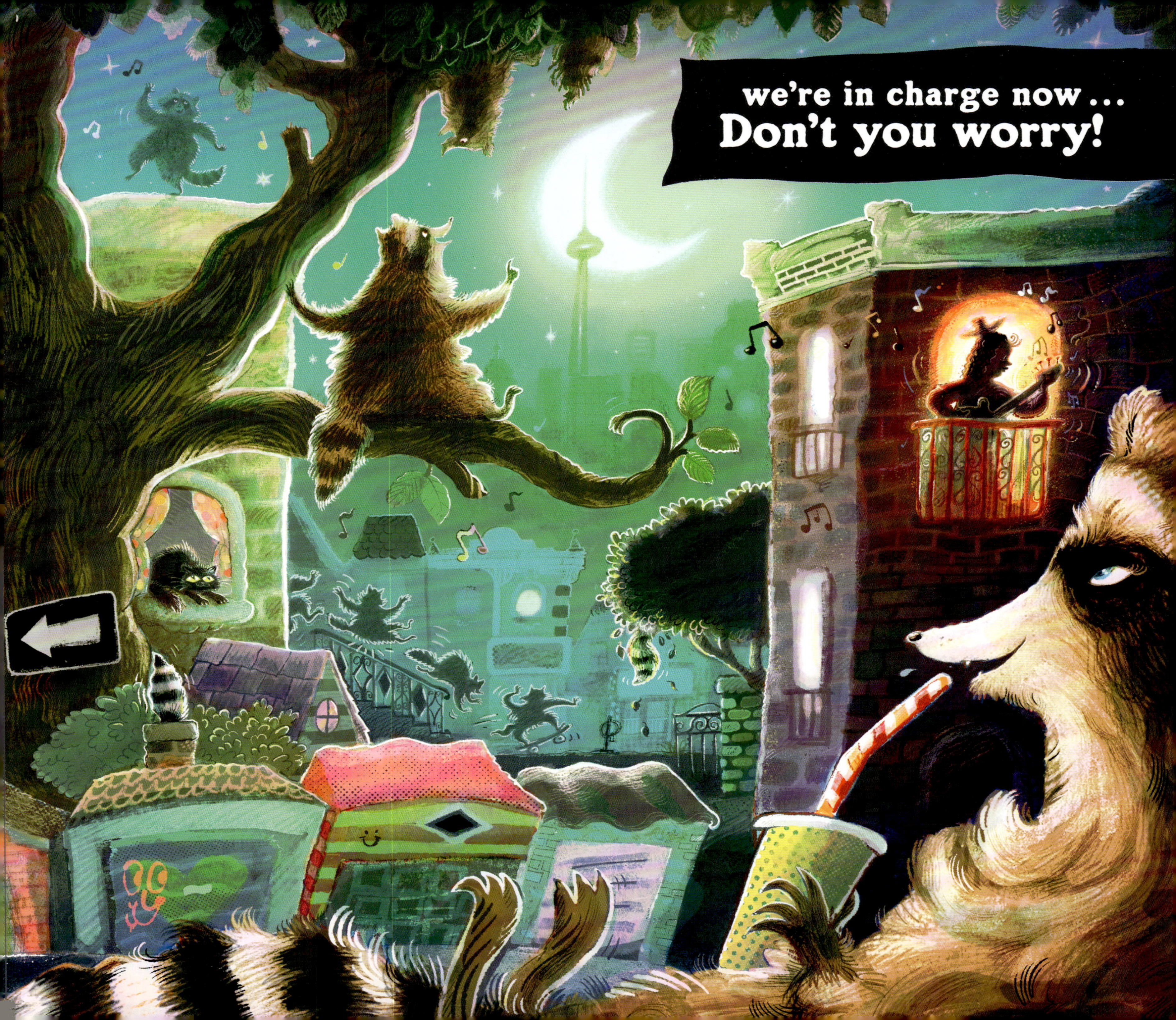

we're in charge now . . .
Don't you worry!

Thank you Juliana Neufeld, Adam Holman, Trisha Yeo, Shemeena Shraya, Derritt Mason, Rachel Letofsky, Karen Li, Karen Boersma, Sarah Howden, Alisa Baldwin, and everyone at Owlkids —V.S.

To my dearest mum. Thank you for seeing and loving me as I am —J.N.

Text © 2022 Vivek Shraya | Illustrations © 2022 Juliana Neufeld

All rights reserved. No part of this publication may be reproduced, stored in a retrieval system, or transmitted in any form or by any means, without the prior written permission of Owlkids Books Inc., or in the case of photocopying or other reprographic copying, a license from the Canadian Copyright Licensing Agency (Access Copyright). For an Access Copyright license, visit www.accesscopyright.ca or call toll-free to 1-800-893-5777.

Owlkids Books acknowledges the financial support of the Canada Council for the Arts, the Ontario Arts Council, the Government of Canada through the Canada Book Fund (CBF) and the Government of Ontario through the Ontario Creates Book Initiative for our publishing activities.

Published in Canada by Owlkids Books Inc., 1 Eglinton Avenue East, Toronto, ON M4P 3A1 | Published in the US by Owlkids Books Inc., 1700 Fourth Street, Berkeley, CA 94710

Library of Congress Control Number: 2021951812

Library and Archives Canada Cataloguing in Publication

Title: Revenge of the raccoons / written by Vivek Shraya ; illustrated by Juliana Neufeld.
Names: Shraya, Vivek, 1981- author. | Neufeld, Juliana, 1982- illustrator.
Identifiers: Canadiana 20210389575 | ISBN 9781771474382 (hardcover)
Classification: LCC PS8637.H73 R48 2022 | DDC jC813/.6—dc23

Edited by Karen Li and Sarah Howden | Designed by Alisa Baldwin

Manufactured in Shenzhen, Guangdong, China, in April 2022, by C&C Offset
Job #HV7823

A   B   C   D   E   F

Publisher of Chirp, Chickadee and OWL
www.owlkidsbooks.com | Owlkids Books is a division of bayard canada | ONTARIO ARTS COUNCIL / CONSEIL DES ARTS DE L'ONTARIO   Canada Council for the Arts / Conseil des Arts du Canada   Canada